Tell Me You're Mine

MELODY RAINNE

About the Author

Melody Rainne is a new romance author who lives in a small town in Michigan's Upper Peninsula. She is married to her husband of eight years and has two children.

One

THE ATMOSPHERE in this restaurant is everything you'd imagine it to be on Valentine's Day. It was already filled with happy couples, lovingly staring into each other's eyes, as if nothing else mattered in the world. Each candlelit table was small, intimate. Only seating two. The red tablecloths draped over them matched my dress, and I wished I had chosen another color to wear this evening. I was nervous enough about tonight that I honestly just chose the first dress I happened to grab out of my closet. I was never really confident with the way I chose to dress for a date on a normal day. But this was different.

My best friend Quinn said she was sick and tired of hearing me complain about being single, so she has the brilliant idea of setting me up with someone. She promised that he was absolutely perfect for me and that I'd fall in love with him at first sight. I checked my watch, noting the time. My date was currently 40 minutes late. I looked all over the restaurant, trying my best not to appear as desperate as I felt.

No sign of him. Everyone was already seated and

enjoying their dinner, as well as the company seated across from them. No one was standing near the door looking for me. There were a couple of men sitting up at the bar that appeared to be by themselves, but they were all nursing beers and watching whatever was on the television set up behind the bar. No one was looking for their date there either.

My heart began to pound, and I could feel heat creeping up the back of my neck. I'm sure any second now my face would match the tablecloths.

"Can I get you anything to drink to start off with?" A waiter appeared out of nowhere.

"A glass of wine, please."

"Would you like a copy of our wine list to look at, or do you already have a blend in mind?"

"Any will do, really," I smiled up at him sadly. He was a younger man, with kind eyes. "Surprise me, please."

He nodded. "You got it. I'll be right back with it."

I nodded to myself as he walked away. Glancing once more towards the door, I hoped to see the man that would save me from my humiliation. I was not so lucky.

A blind date.

On Valentine's day.

Who does that? Why did I ever think this was a good idea? I shouldn't have gone along with it. I should have just told Quinn how stupid of an idea I thought this was.

Instead, I told her that I'd love to go. That it was a great idea. Meeting a man for the very first time, out to dinner, on the most romantic day of the year. What could possibly go wrong?

Well, everything apparently. Here I was, in the center of a sea of happy couples, alone with my heart breaking. Not that I expected my date to be 'the one' or anything like that.

I am just fed up with all the bad luck I have been experiencing in the realm of dating.

Just then the waiter returned with my wine.

"I do hope this is to your liking," he said as he handed me the glass.

I laughed, thinking he sounded sort of like a character from a television show. I took a sip. "It's delicious, thank you." It really was.

"If you would like, I can bring you out the rest of the bottle."

"I would love that, thank you." He was quickly becoming my new best friend.

As I slowly drained the rest of the bottle of wine I debated on whether to just pack it up and leave or stay and have one more glass. Or bottle. Going home to an empty house didn't really sound all that appealing. Sure, sitting in a restaurant filled with happy couples was depressing, but going home alone sounded so much worse.

"Excuse me," a voice came from my left. "I couldn't help but notice that you were alone."

Very observant of you, I thought. I turned to see a man standing next to me. Blinking a few times, I looked harder, making sure he was real. I had never seen someone so perfect in my life. His sharp jawline, perfect amount of stubble, his brown hair looking so soft, and feathery, it made you want to run your hands through it. He was dressed up in a suit, which hung perfectly off his broad shoulders.

"Am I bothering you?" The man asked.

Shit. I was staring. Great first impression, Lexi.

"I'm sorry," I said, shaking my head. Embarrassment crept up the back of my neck. "No, no. Of course you're not bothering me. I was just . . . distracted." By your sexiness.

The man laughed. It was a beautiful sound. "I'm Brody," he said as he offered me his hand. I slowly took it in mine.

"Lexi."

Two

"WELL, Lexi. What is a beautiful woman like you doing here alone on Valentine's Day?"

Smooth.

"I wasn't supposed to be alone," I admitted. "I was supposed to be here on a date. A . . . blind date." I swallowed hard. I don't know why the fact that I was on a blind date was so embarrassing to me. I guess because it made it sound like I wasn't able to get a man on my own. Well, I wasn't, but having been set up on a blind date screamed to the world that you sucked in the romantic department enough that someone felt the need to step in and help you out.

Brody looked around the restaurant. "I'm guessing he was a no-show."

"Good guess."

"I am so sorry," his tone changed. He didn't sound like he pitied me though. He actually sounded a little concerned. It was sweet.

"I see you have already polished off an entire bottle of wine," he laughed. I loved that there was no judgement in his voice. "But may I buy you just one more glass? No one should be alone on the most romantic day of the year." His smile could melt even the coldest of hearts.

"Sure," I smiled brightly. "One more couldn't hurt."

Brody flagged down our watier and ordered us both a fresh glass of wine as he took a seat across from me. One glass turned into another bottle.

At first I wasn't sure about this, but as the evening wore on I grew more and more comfortable around Brody. It was almost as if I traded one blind date for another. After a while I found myself forgetting about the humiliation of being stood up and began to enjoy myself.

We talked about everything under the sun, as long as it wasn't too personal. Early on we decided to keep things casual. Just two lonely people sharing a few drinks. Nothing more.

Worked for me.

Three

THAT PLAN DIDN'T WORK. Brody and I talked for hours, sharing stories of our lives and getting to know a bit about each other. Before I knew it I was in my car following him home.

The second we arrived at his house, Brody dragged me off to his bedroom. Not that there really was any dragging. I was more than willing to follow that man.

"You sure this is what you want?" He asks, pausing just outside his bedroom door.

"Very sure," I said, breathlessly.

The look in his eyes was intoxicating. He pulled me into his room, grabbing me by the waist and tossing me onto his bed. Slowly, he climbs on top of me. Grabbing the back of my head, he pulled me to him, kissing me passionately. I can't remember the last time I was kissed like this. Or if I ever was at all.

It was thrilling.

Suddenly, he pulls back, leaving me breathless. Brody begins kissing my neck, leading a slow, burning trail down my body. As he gets to my thighs, he alternates from kisses to light nibbles.

He looks up into my eyes before going back down. The second our gazes connect I feel a jolt of electricity throughout my entire body. Using only his tongue, he flicks it up and down and I moan in pleasure. Grabbing my waist again, he pulls me even closer.

I run my fingers through his hair, lightly grabbing a handful to push his face deeper between my legs. As I get closer to the edge, Brody stops, crawling back on top of me. With a low growl in the back of his throat, he kisses me hard, teasing me with just the tip. He doesn't go in, continuing to rub up against my opening.

The pleasure is building, the anticipation almost too much. "Please," I beg. "I need you." I arch my back, ready for him. All of him.

With one thrust, he buries himself deep inside me. I cry out in ecstasy. As he begins to move in and out, I wrap my legs tightly around his body.

He's not going anywhere.

I rake my hands down his back, moaning his name. With my legs still wrapped around him, Brody stands up. As he kisses me deeply he pushes my back against the wall and fucks me hard.

As he thrusts away, getting deeper and deeper inside me, he whispers, "I love the way you feel, wrapped around me like this."

With his words I cry out, the orgasm ripping through me. We both collapse on the bed, exhausted and out of breath.

"That was . . ."

"Amazing?" Brody asked, rolling on his side to face me better.

I nodded. "So amazing." I leaned over and kissed him. He deepened the kiss, pulling my body closer to his. I could feel the heat coming off him, and in that moment, I never wanted him to let me go.

I know this was just a one-nighter, and that I shouldn't get attached. I had absolutely no plans of doing that either. This moment, here, right here in his arms, was absolutely perfect.

Brody held me close, and I fell asleep in the comfort of his arms.

Tonight had turned out even better than I imagined. I only hope I'll be able to remember it in the morning.

Four

I WOKE up the next morning hungover and a little confused. I knew where I was and what had happened last night. That wasn't something I was going to be forgetting about for a long time. What I didn't know was why I was feeling the way I did. I felt happy, I felt content. I felt like . . . I already wanted to see Brody again. I needed to. Even though he was sleeping in the bed right next to me, I knew I wanted to see him again.

But this was not at all in our plans - my sudden feelings. They took hold by surprise and I wasn't exactly sure what to do about them.

It has to be the alcohol talking, I think to myself. There's no other explanation. I was upset about being stood up, drank way more than I intended to, and had a great time with a total stranger. That was it. Nothing more, nothing less. Later on when I was no longer feeling the effects of the alcohol, I'd feel normal again about this situation.

I looked over at him, still asleep. He had his mouth

closed and was snoring softly. His hair was sticking out in all directions.

Damn. He was hot even as he slept.

I moved slowly, trying not to wake him up. I grabbed my clothes that were scattered around the room and my purse and headed for the door. Before softly closing the door to Brody's bedroom, I snuck one last look at the man.

Sigh. It was a shame I'd never get that sexy man ever again. I just knew I'd be thinking about him all the way home.

As I hopped out of the car I was greeted to the sight of my best friend sitting on my front porch steps, coffees in hand.

Thank God for Quinn.

"Well, well, well." She says with a smirk, looking me up and down. I was tempted to hop back in my car and drive away. "What do we have here? Same exact outfit as last night. Only your hair is tangled and your makeup is a bit runny," she pointed near the corner of her eye, dragging her finger down her face to tell me that I had mascara running down my own face.

I really, really wanted to turn around and get back in my car, or that the ground would open up and swallow me whole. I'd welcome either option at this point.

"So," she pressed when I still hadn't said anything to her. "I take it you had an amazing time on your blind date. You can totally thank me for that later," she said, handing me one of the cups of coffee.

"Um, not exactly." I stared at the coffee in my hands, feeling my face and neck warming up even though I hadn't even taken a sip yet. It was way too early to be having this type of conversation. I was really hoping to at least have a few hours to myself to process all that happened. I don't even know how I was feeling about all this myself.

Quinn cocked an eyebrow at me. "So you didn't have a good time with Tom?" She asked, clearly confused. From the state of me you'd think we had a great time.

"Well, I might have. If he had even bothered to show up."

"I'm sorry, what?"

I nodded. "Yeah. Your so-called perfect man never showed up. Stood me up." I complained as I unlocked my front door, gesturing for her to come on inside. Although she could have just come in by herself before I even arrived, We each had a spare key to the other's house in case of emergencies. That's how close we were. There wasn't a single thing we didn't know about each other.

Except each other's definition of 'perfect man' apparently.

"What do you mean, he never showed?"

I shrugged. "Just that - he never showed up to our date. I sat in that restaurant by myself, waiting. It was humiliating."

"Aw, babe. I'm so sorry. I really thought he'd be the one for you."

I shrugged again as I plopped down next to her on the couch. "It's all right." I sipped my coffee, never taking my eyes off it. I still wasn't sure I was ready to have this conversation.

"Okay," she said, sipping her own coffee. "Wait a minute!" She slapped her hand down on the decorative pillow next to her. "You came home in the same clothes as yesterday, looking pretty disheveled," she narrowed her eyes at me. "So . . . spill."

I sighed heavily. Knowing Quinn, she was never going

to let this go until she got enough details to satisfy her curiosity.

"So basically the lovely gentleman you set me up with never showed. There were no calls, no texts, nothing to even let me know either. So I sat alone, for what felt like forever, surrounded by happy couples."

"That sounds awful. I'm so sorry."

"It was absolutely humiliating. So anyway, after sitting there for a while, looking pathetic and finishing off a bottle of the best wine I have ever tasted, a man comes over and we talk. Oh, the wine was suggested to me by the waiter, who is now my new best friend," I informed her.

Quinn shot me a hurt look.

"Sorry," I shrugged, "but he didn't set me up on the world's worst blind date."

"True."

"Well anyway, so this new guy comes over and introduces himself. He joined me for a glass of wine, which turned into a few glasses of wine, and then I . . . went home with him."

I snuck a look at Quinn, who had been just sitting there silently, her mouth hanging wide open. I'd have to admit, it wasn't her best look. "Well, say something," I let out a small laugh. "You're making me feel awkward."

Quinn shook her head. "I don't know what to say," she admitted. Well this was a first. "This isn't like you. In fact, it's like, the complete opposite."

"It is?"

"Well yeah. "The Lexi I know would never just go home with a guy. Especially one she'd just met." It was weird to hear her talk about me like that.

My face was now on fire. She wasn't wrong though. This was completely out of character for me.

"So why did you?" She asked.

"I don't know," I answered honestly. "There was just something about him."

"I'm sure there was," she teased.

"No, not that," I laughed. Although, I did enjoy that. A lot. "I don't know how to describe it, really."

"Well, I, for one, am glad you're finally letting your hair down and having fun. Lord knows you need it. Are you going to see him again? Please say you're going to see him again."

"I'm not sure."

"Oh. Well, what did he say when he texted you last?"

"He didn't."

"Alright, what about your last call?"

I shrugged. "We didn't exchange numbers."

"How on earth do you have drinks with a hot guy - I'm assuming he's hot, go home with him, and not get his number?"

"We agreed that it was supposed to just be a one-time thing." I shrugged again.

"Two lonely people spending Valentine's Day together and never seeing each other again. It's kind of sweet," she said, a dreamy look appearing in her eyes. "It actually sounds quite romantic."

Romantic? I don't know about that. Hot and steamy was more like it.

"Well, anyway, I'm glad things worked out for you. Even if I am a little jealous," she sat back on the couch, pretending to pout.

Five

I WAS KICKING myself for not getting Brody's phone number. Yeah, I know, we agreed to it being just one night. But lately, I haven't been able to get him off my mind. Every day, all I could think about was him.

I wondered what he was doing. If he even thought about me at all. I hoped so. It turns out I didn't want just sex, not with Brody. Although I'd gladly participate in that again. I wanted to be near him. I really wanted to get to know him and spend time with him.

A lot more time. I couldn't even look him up in the phone book if I wanted to either.

Wait, do people even still use those anymore?

As part of our weird little agreement, last names weren't exchanged either. Just the basic facts - first names and the fact that we were both alone on what was supposed to be the most romantic day of the year.

Sigh . . . if only I knew just one piece of information about the man that could help me find him.

He did take me to his house though! If only I could remember where that was. I know I'm starting to sound a little creepy and stalkerish, but I promise, I'm not. I just couldn't help it. I can't get him off my mind, and it's driving me nuts.

There's gotta be a reason, right? We couldn't just end with a one-night stand.

I wanted more. I only hoped that he did too.

I wracked my brain for hours, trying to remember any and all details that I could about where Brody lived. I should have paid more attention when I left the morning after. I was hungover and still a little humiliated from being stood up that I just booked it out of there as fast as I could.

I decided that driving back to the restaurant where we met was going to be my best bet. From there I should be able to retrace my steps and hopefully find my way back to Brody's.

It only took me a couple of wrong turns, but I finally pulled up in front of the house I believed to be his. The back Silverado parked in the driveway looked like his. It was clean and shiny, looking all brand new. I've seen a few of these same trucks around town, but only Brody kept his in pristine condition.

As I stepped out of the car I closed the door softly, making as little noise as possible. I was quickly losing the small amount of confidence that I had built up on the way here.

What if he didn't want me here? What if he came out of the door screaming at me to leave? Maybe he hadn't had as good a time as I did. Perhaps he thought I was bad in bed . . .

So many horrible thoughts rushing through my head at the moment. I squeezed my eyes shut, trying to rid myself of all the doubt that had somehow come crashing down on me.

"This could be considered stalking, you know."

Shit.

My eyes flew open and I was greeted to the sight of Brody standing on his front porch, one hand still on the door knob, the other holding his keys. He was wearing a business suit and he looked freshly showered. His hair was slightly damp but neat. I wanted to run my hands through it.

Ged, this man is sexy.

"I'm, I'm sorry," I stuttered. My chest burned with embarrassment, even though the playful smirk on his face let me know he was joking.

He closed his front door the rest of the way and checked that it was locked before walking down and stopping right in front of me. "What are you doing here?" He asked. He didn't sound upset or angry that some random one-night stand had just shown up at his house. Unannounced and uninvited. So that was good.

But, now the moment I had been waiting for was here. "I wanted to see you. I've been wanting to see you," I admitted, managing to look him in the eyes.

That sexy smile appeared again. "You have?"

All I could manage to do was nod.

"Well, he said, "I'm glad. Because I wanted to see you again as well."

My heart stopped. "Really?"

"Really," he smiled. "I've been beating myself up about not getting your number that night. I know, it was my idea not to exchange them in the first place. But there's just something incredible about you, Lexi. I want more of you. And I don't just mean the sexy time. Although . . ." he smirked, causing my face to burn hotter.

Brody laughed, and I loved the sound of it. I loved

everything about him. Well, maybe love was too strong a word, but you know what I mean.

"So you'd be open to seeing me again?"

"I would love to see you again," he took a step towards me. His voice right now was low and husky, driving shivers throughout my body. "So let me give you my number this time and we can make a date."

I nodded again, handing him my phone. I didn't care about the goofy smile on my face as he punched in his number.

"Here you go," he said as he handed it back to me.

I shot him a quick text, just containing my name. "Now you have mine too."

He laughed. "About time." Brody checked his watch. "I have to head in to work, but how about tomorrow night you come back here and I can cook you dinner?"

"I'd love that." I honestly can't remember the last time that a man offered to cook for me. "Um, should I bring anything?"

"Just your sexy self," he said with a wink. "I'll see you tomorrow."

"I can't wait," I said before hopping into my car so he could get to work.

I drove home with the biggest smile on my face. I couldn't wait to tell Quinn all about this.

TO SAY I was nervous would be an understatement. The first time Brody and I were together was because we were both just two lonely people who happened to be in the same place at the same time. And we were both completely wasted.

This time it was planned, and we were sober. I had no idea why this fact made me so damn nervous. Maybe it had something to do with the fact that this was my first real date in God knows how long.

At least one with a man that'll actually show up.

He'll show up, right? It's not like he'd actually ditch me at his own house.

I hoped.

His truck was in the driveway when I pulled up and there seemed to be lights on in the house.

That was a good sign.

I carefully got out of the car, making sure not to ruin my new dress. I swear, the second I told Quinn about tonight, she dragged me to the mall, saying I needed the perfect outfit and that she knew just where to find it.

I hated shopping, especially for clothes, but one look in my closet and I agreed, I could use something new. I didn't have anything remotely sexy looking in there. Well, maybe the dress I wore on Valentine's Day, but come on. You can't wear the same thing for two dates in a row. Not that the first time was really a date, but still.

The dress she picked out was unlike anything I've ever worn. I mean, I would never in a million years have picked this out for myself. But Quinn made me try it on and insisted that I looked hot and that Brosy wouldn't be able to take his hands off me.

It was form-fitting, hugging my body in all the right places. It had long sleeves, was cut in a v-shape that came to just under my chest, and the entire thing came to a stop just a few inches under my booty. One wrong move and Brody would be getting a free show. To top it off the dress had buttons all the way down the front.

This dress had one thing on its mind and one thing only.

Smoothing it down the best I could, I headed up the porch steps to knock on the door.

When Brody answered, he immediately raked his eyes up and down my body. There's no way he couldn't see my embarrassment which was sure to stand out against the black fabric of the dress. "Wow," he breathed. "You look . . ."

Ridiculous?" I offered.

"Amazing," he corrected me. "Come on in." He held the door for me as I walked in and looked around the familiar living room.

"Dinner smells delicious," I said, setting my purse on his coffee table.

"It's just about finished if you'd like to follow me into

the kitchen," he smiled. I'd gladly follow that man anywhere. "Take a seat," he said as he handed me a glass of wine.

"Oh!" I exclaimed as I sat down at the table and got a good look at it.

"Do you like it?" Brody asked.

He had recreated the table from the restaurant the night we met. It was the sweetest thing anyone has ever done for me. "I love it." His eyes sparkled as he smiled.

Brody was sweet, sexy, and seemed to like me. This man was full of surprises.

We ate slowly, taking our time to talk and get to know each other. And I have to admit, the more I learned about Brody, the more I began to find myself falling for him.

If we hadn't met already I'd be calling this a classic case of love at first sight. The night was already everything I had always dreamed a first date would be,

It was absolutely perfect.

He was perfect. And I never wanted this to end.

After dinner we took our wine and sat down in front of the fire he had going. It took a little maneuvering but I managed to find a position on the floor cushions that was both somewhat comfortable and not having me popping out everywhere.

"That . . . looks uncomfortable," Broday said after a minute, nodding to my dress. "Don't get me wrong," he put his hands up in defense. "It's a beautiful dress and you look sexy as hell in it. It just doesn't seem to be all that comfortable."

"It's not," I laughed. "It's really not, at all. A friend suggested that I wear it and wouldn't take no for an answer."

"Well, she was right. You look stunning," he said.

"Thank you." I didn't know what else to say. The wine didn't seem to be doing its job of giving me false confidence and I was still feeling a bit shy.

Why did I feel like this around him? Unlike the dress, he didn't make me feel uncomfortable. He made my heart beat wildly, when he kissed me I felt a bit lightheaded - in a good way.

And what was I supposed to say to him anyways? You look good too? Because let's face it, he always did.

"If you wanted, I could help you out with that." Brody's voice brought me back from out of my own head.

"I . . . what?" I asked, confused. My face burned with more than the heat from the flames.

"Your dress. Wouldn't it be more comfortable . . . off?" he asked, arching an eyebrow.

"I . . ." Oh. Oh, yes. Yes it would.

I nodded slowly and Brody set our wine glasses on the table, scooting closer to me. He leaned over and kissed the top of my shoulder, sending shivers down my spine. "Are you sure this is okay?" he asked before continuing.

"Very sure," I answered breathlessly. I could see the passion in his eyes as he gently placed his hands on either side of my face, pulling me in for a kiss. I moaned against him as he deepened the kiss.

His hands moved down the buttons on my dress. And slowly, one by one, he began to undo them.

"Uh, uh," I shook my head. "Don't be gentle, with the dress or with me."

He cocked an eyebrow.

"I'm sure," I answered his silent question.

In one swift movement, Brody had all the buttons undone. Impressively, not a single one had popped off. As he sled the dress off my shoulders I worked on the buttons on his own shirt. I slid it off of him, running my hands over his smooth, muscular chest and rock hard abs.

And speaking of rock hard, I could see that Brody was all ready for me.

And I was more than ready for him.

We both quickly finished undressing and he laid me down, crawling on top of me. The glow of the fireplace made him seem almost ethereal. The sight of him left me breathless.

Brody ran a hand through my hair. "You are gorgeous."

I looked into his eyes, biting my bottom lip. "Take me," I told him. "I need you. I need to feel you."

I barely got the words out before he crushed his mouth on mine. I raised my hips up to meet him, at the same time reaching down to grasp his massive erection, guiding him into me.

With one thrust he buried himself deep inside me, and I cried out. I wrapped my legs around his strong body, urging him closer to me as he continued thrusting in and out.

He kissed me deeply, passionately as one hand cupped my breast, stroking his thumb over my erect nipple. The sensation caused me to moan under him.

We continued moving rhythmically together, going faster and faster, until I couldn't take it anymore. I cried out his name as the orgasm ripped through me.

Brody soon followed. His body trembled as he gave one last, long, hard thrust. Panting, he rolled off and laid down next to me, placing a kiss on my shoulder. We both laid there, relishing in the pleasure and letting the fire warm our naked bodies.

"How do you feel?" he asked gently, grabbing my hand.

I turned to face him. "Amazing. I feel amazing."

"I'm glad," he smiled, reaching over to kiss me. "I do too."

"I don't want to get up," he laughed.

"I don't think I can."

"That good, huh?" he winked.

I nodded once. "That good."

We laid here, in each other's arms in front of the roaring fire, for quite some time. Neither of us wanting to let the other go.

"If you could have one wish," Brody kissed the top of my head, "what would it be?"

"Easy," I tilted my head up to look in his eyes. "Tell me you're mine."

www.ingramcontent.com/pod-product-compliance
Lightning Source LLC
Chambersburg PA
CBHW031453310726
48971CB00003B/903